ELKBAR

written by Taylor Mosbey
and illustrated by Chris Fason

To James, Marian, and John,
My love for you is bigger than Really Big Mountain.
To all Friends of Elkbar,
You are extraordinary
-t.m.

penguintonia.com

First Edition, October 2023

Elkbar was an extraordinary penguin.

He had a twin turbo rocket pack.

He had a thermonuclear refrigerator ray.

He also had a digital watch.

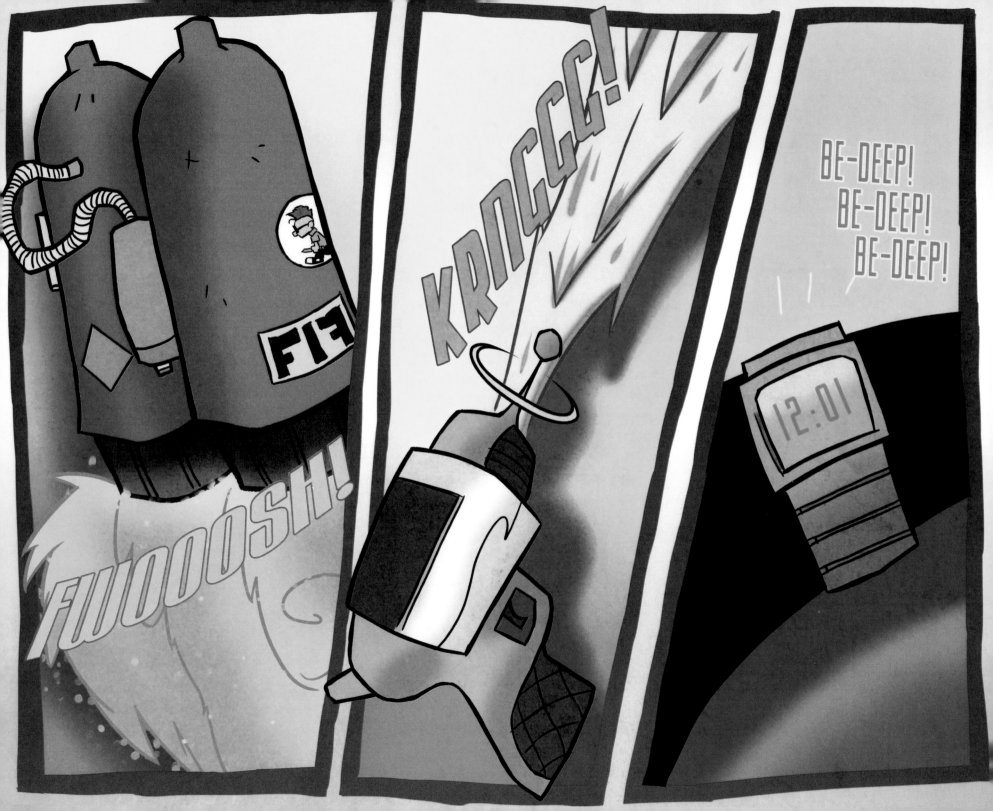

All the other penguins were jealous of the cool stuff he had.

Elkbar was sad because although he had cool stuff
he had no friends, and no matter how nice he was
he could never get the other penguins to like him.
He did try to make some friends out of snow,
but they weren't any good.

They couldn't play or talk.

They couldn't even do advanced calculus.

Elkbar had no clue what he could do to become friends with other penguins, but he knew of someone who might know:

"The great and powerful Fargo Roberts, Wise Moose of the Far East."

He packed some sandwiches and Elkbar began his journey. After many miles he finally reached the bottom of "Really Big Mountain."

He looked up in awe and wondered how long it would take to climb.

Days? Months? Years?

Luckily Elkbar had his rocket pack
and it only took him roughly 7.06285 seconds.

"Hello, Fargo Roberts," said Elkbar after he'd reached the top.

"Who is that?" asked Fargo Roberts in a wise and raspy voice, "I can't see."

"It is only I, Elkbar the penguin," said Elkbar.

"Oh," said Fargo, "What's shaking?"

"Not much," Elkbar said, "I just need to ask you something…"

"I don't validate parking," said Fargo interrupting.

"No, no, it's not that. It's…"

"Are you gonna ask why I'm blind?" asked Fargo, interrupting again,
"Because I can tell you now that I'm not really blind.
I just took a vow of blindness."

Elkbar tried to explain again, "No, it's not that either. It's just - "

"Well what is it?" Fargo interrupted yet another time.

"You sure interrupt a lot," said Elkbar in amazement.

"Yeah, sorry, you'll have to forgive me,
I can't see when you're talking," said Fargo.

Elkbar paused for a moment then asked,
"I need to know how to make friends with the other penguins."

Fargo tried to rest his chin on his hoof, but he missed the first time (because, you know, he can't see).

But after a second, his chin was resting nicely on his hoof, and he said, "Hmm... this problem baffles me."

He thought and thought and it looked as if he would never come up with an answer. But then he jumped up with enlightenment! "I've got it! You could make new friends... out of snow!"

"I already tried that and it didn't work," said Elkbar sadly.

"Hmm," mumbled Fargo. "Have you tried being nice?"
he asked hopefully.

"Yes," Elkbar nodded.

"Oh," said Fargo,
"I guess I could just give you a bottle of my patented
'Become My Friend Because You Have No Reason Not To' potion."

Elkbar leaped with excitement,
"That would be great! How much will it cost me?"

"It's free... with a five dollar donation," said Fargo.

"Woobitypoob!" exclaimed Elkbar.

Elkbar made a quick stop at the gift shop,
made his donation, got the potion and also a nifty t-shirt,
and then was on his way home to Penguintonia
(which is where the penguins live, obviously).

But on his flight back something unexpected happened!
Big Zombie Japanese Beetles from Denmark attacked
him with slingshots.

Elkbar swooped and swerved in the sky, and did a very good job of dodging all the rocks, but those beetles were right on his little tail.

Just as Elkbar was about to escape a rock hit the potion bottle!
It broke! And every last drop spilled out.

Oh, how Elkbar was so sad. He thought he might fly back to Fargo and get another, but all of that fancy flying nearly emptied the fuel tank. He only had enough to make it home.

In fact he only barely had enough to make it home.

His descent was a bit awkward, but he managed to land safely, although he had to walk quite a ways to get to town. When he finally did arrive at the border he noticed something was not right. Some of the buildings were on fire!

Elkbar was amazed and a little frightened because he had never seen buildings made of ice on fire.

To be certain Elkbar had never seen anything made of ice on fire.

Luckily he was a good shot, and with his thermonuclear
refrigerator ray he was able to freeze the fire.

Frozen fire was another thing Elkbar had never seen,
but he was very delighted the fires were put out.

He expected all his fellow penguins to come out from hiding and scoop
him up on their small shoulders with great cheering
...but it never happened. There was not a penguin in sight.
There was nothing.

"They must be in Town Square," Elkbar thought out loud, waddling quickly toward that direction.

As he did he heard noises, but not the noises of penguins.

No, these noises were of something meaner than Mr. Wister, the meanest penguin around.

The closer and closer he got to Town Square the louder and louder the sounds grew. Elkbar saw flashes of fiery light bursting around a corner and then he saw all the penguins gathered in a big scared group.

But then he saw what they were scared of;
a dangerous looking robot lion creature!

"ROARzbbbt!" the big cat thing roared,
"Prepare for the long journey, pathetic pzzz-enguins."

Elkbar watched as the penguins cowered.

"You will all be my slaves and do all sorts of th-zzzz-ings for me!
Like my laundry! And also build me a shrine!
Bzzret... for I am the Great and Powerful
BOB the Robo-Lyon!"

fig 4A

It all came together inside of Elkbar's brain.

This creature, this Bob the Robo-Lyon, was evil
and Elkbar would have none of it.

He at once forgot how he wanted to be liked by the penguins.
He didn't care if none ever would.

This menace must be stopped at all costs!

The penguins of Penguintonia were his people and he would
do everything in his power to save them.

In a flash he jumped onto the statue of Old Jacobin Coldnasal
(the founder of Penguintonia) and he yelled in a great penguin voice,
"Hey, you! Bobby Lyon!
You aren't taking anybody anywhere!"

Bob turned, shocked, to face Elkbar,
"Who dares confront me and call me Bobby?
I detest that name ever-szzert so much!"

"It is only I, Elkbar the penguin," said Elkbar confidently.

"Well, Elkbar, prepare to be made into an example sandwich!
You will taste the power of my fire bolts!"
and with that, Bob shot two flaming balls of fire at Elkbar.

Elkbar's eyes widened, but he was able to fire his ray
and the balls of fire turned into balls of ice.

"No thanks, Bobby boy," said Elkbar, "I'm not hungry."

Now it was Bob's eyes that widened.
"I can't be-zz-lieve you d-rz-id that!" roared Bob,
and he leapt into the air to attack Elkbar
with his giant sharp robo-teeth glimmering.

"Believe it," said Elkbar, "Also you better believe this, too."

And Elkbar fired a blast from his ray
which hit mean Bob Robo-Lyon.
He froze and fell down in a mighty crash,
and he broke into hundreds of pieces.

But everyone noticed something bizarre.
There was a fluffy mound of black fuzz amongst the debris.
A very dizzy looking kitten sat
trying to collect his wits.

He shook his head then jumped up into the air,
and from his backpack
(which was too small to notice when he was sitting)
a propeller whirled out and began to carry the kitten away.

The kitten shook his fist at Elkbar!

"You haven't seen the last of me, Elkbar!" yelled the kitten
in a cute little kitten voice,
"I'll be back for you and all your fellow penguins!
I'll come back with a better robot suit!
You will all be mine!"

So with a few evil, but adorable,
kitty laughs, the kitten was carried away.

Once things got settled all the penguins felt
pretty bad for not being Elkbar's friend.

They were ashamed of their jealousy,
and they knew Elkbar could have run away to
save his own tail-feathers, but he didn't.

Elkbar had saved the day.
The penguins begged for
his forgiveness,
and he happily forgave them.

He finally had friends, and he was pretty happy,
but he knew that Bob was out there
and must be brought to justice,
and if he wasn't stopped he'd hurt others.
So Elkbar set out to find him,
and along the way he had many crazy adventures
and met new friends...

But those are stories for other times.

Mister Wister   Burden   Murphy   Penelope the Great   Swoozan   Asher

JACS   Jilpat   Lulabell   Monroe   Zebulon   Niko

In 2002 I found myself in Sand City, Ca investigating some very neat artisan shops with my father. One in particular had a mass of old plaster molds, and amongst these underappreciated dusty relics was a solitary lovably lopsided penguin. Without hesitating, my father snatched it up as a present for me, and before we left the shop I'd named him Elkbar. Or maybe that's what he told me his name was. Regardless, after many moves since, he always has a place on my shelf. Currently, he guards my vinyl records.

Not long after I found Elkbar I was given a college assignment of writing a short story. Although it's voice was slightly more in the style of a yarn-spinning story teller, the story I wrote then was the story of our dear Elkbar in this book. I knew I must make the tale into a kids' book and I thought I'd illustrate it. I got half-way through the first piece, a water color of Elkbar, and thought maybe I shouldn't illustrate the book. When I was finished I was more than convinced. So I began a long (way longer than 7.06285 seconds) journey to find the right person to give Elkbar the wings he needed to fly. I mean that figuratively; penguins don't fly. Naturally.

In 2008, after finding and losing artists, all with great and different looks for our hero, I found that person in Chris Fason, and he was all in! Mostly. He loved the project, but had family to feed and bills to pay, and I just didn't have the resources to compensate him for his time. Elkbar was on the backburner, but ever in our minds.

Then crowd funding became a thing. It became the way to make this happen, and in 2012 we raised the money to get "Elkbar" printed! 136 backers, more than a few complete strangers, gave us what we needed to print 500 copies of the book in January of 2013. I won't name all of them here, but I will mention below those who, as a backer reward, named the penguins on the previous page. I have hopes their contributions will last in upcoming Elkbar tales.

Ten years have passed since Elkbar debuted in print, and I've only a small handful, personal copies, of those original 500 books. Life has had joys and pains, ups and downs, and failures and accomplishments, but those who've been friends of Elkbar have never stopped loving the story, and have encouraged me (sometimes very vocally) to write more of Elkbar's journeys. I will.

But first I want to re-release this book to a larger audience, and to more friends for Elkbar. This book is nearly identical to the 2013 book, with minor art changes, and a smattering of changes to the text. Moving forward, the format, art, and style may change, much like the look of Elkbar did from artist to artist, but at the heart of it will always be the original Elkbar.

Much Love,
taylor mosbey
October 13, 2023

Mister Wister **Barb Piña**
Jacs **The Baker Family**
Burden **The Brinkman Family**
Jilpat **Ninna**
Murphy **Sandra Kreisle Murphy**
Lulabell **Lauren Payne**

Penelope the Great **Jen Acree & Bryce Elliot**
Monroe **The children of GELi, INC. Monroe County, MS**
Swoozan **The Scarboro Family**
Zebulon **John Mosbey**
Asher **Michael Albanese**
Niko **J. Nathan Poe**

Milton Keynes UK
Ingram Content Group UK Ltd.
UKRC031224021123
431732UK00002B/6